That's Not Goldie!

That's Not Goldie!

By Miriam Schlein • Illustrated by Susan Gough Magurn

SIMON AND SCHUSTER BOOKS FOR YOUNG READERS

Published by Simon & Schuster Inc.

New York • London • Toronto • Sydney • Tokyo • Singapore

SIMON AND SCHUSTER
BOOKS FOR YOUNG READERS
Simon & Schuster Building, Rockefeller Center
1230 Avenue of the Americas, New York, New York 10020

Manufactured in the United States of America

10 9 8 7 6 5 4 3 2 1

Library of Congress Cataloging-in-Publication Data
Schlein, Miriam. That's not Goldie! / by Miriam Schlein ; illustrated by
Susan Magurn. p. cm.
Summary: Benjie's goldfish Goldie, believed to be dead, is flushed down
the toilet and escapes through the sewer system into the goldfish pond at
the Botanical Garden, where she finds a peaceful and happy existence
with others of her kind.
[1. Goldfish—Fiction.] I. Magurn, Susan, ill. II. Title.
PZ7.S347Th 1990 [E]—dc20 90-31560 ISBN 0-671-70005-7

That's Not Goldie!

When Benjie was sick, his
Aunt Margaret gave him a goldfish.
He loved it.
He named it Goldie.

Goldie was special.

She had a little blue dot over her right eye.

"I would know her anywhere," Benjie said.

He liked watching her blow bubbles, and wiggle her tail as she swam.

"Goldie is helping me get better," Benjie said.

One day Goldie just stopped swimming.
She seemed to be just drifting around.
"Hey. Look at that!" Benjie's cousin Milton tapped his finger against the glass.
"She's dead.
Your fish is dead."

Benjie sat up.
"No, she's not! Not Goldie!"
"Well, I guess I have to give her
a burial at sea," said Milton.

"No!" yelled Benjie.

Benjie's cousin Milton picked Goldie up by the tail, dropped her in the toilet, and flushed it.

Benjie had never liked his cousin Milton.

Now he hated him.

Aunt Margaret brought Benjie another goldfish.
"That's not Goldie," Benjie said.
"I don't want it."
He made Aunt Margaret take the fish away.
He pulled the blanket over his head.

Meanwhile, Goldie, who was not dead at all, revived in the cold rushing water.

She swam through the pipes in the house.

These led to bigger pipes, down under the ground.

The big pipes led to a sewer.

Goldie was not the only one down there.

There, in the sewer, were bigger fish.

There were furry rats. There were eels, and some big turtles.

There were men with tools and flashlights in the dark, fixing something.

It was all new to Goldie.

She swam steadily on and came, after some time, to a place where there were two different ways to go.

One way, straight ahead, led to the sewage treatment plant, where all the sludge and muck goes, and gets sorted and skimmed and cleaned, and finally let out into the river. (Of course, Goldie did not know this.)

The other way was through a small pipe that led someplace else. Goldie, being small, took this turn. That was a really lucky decision. You'll see why.

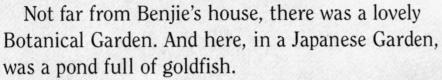

Not far from Benjie's house, there was a lovely
Botanical Garden. And here, in a Japanese Garden,
was a pond full of goldfish.

Goldfish live a long time. As they get older, they
get bigger. And so, in the pond, were many big,
old goldfish. And some smaller ones, too.

Now, it happens that the small pipe where Goldie was swimming led right to this goldfish pond. There was wire mesh blocking the way in and out. But one small part was broken and Goldie, being so small, swam right through.

And soon, there she was, in the goldfish pond of The Botanical Garden, swimming with all the other goldfish, big and small.

Goldie's underground voyage had taken her a week.
For Benjie, it was not a good week. He didn't feel like
eating. Or reading.

"The boy needs an outing," said his grandfather.
"I'm coming to visit, and take him you-know-where."

Benjie's mother did-know-where. She knew her
father's—Benjie's grandfather's—favorite place in the
world was The Botanical Garden, and especially the
goldfish pond.

"It's no good, Dad. He'll just look at those fish and
say, 'That's not Goldie!'"

"We'll see," said Benjie's grandfather.

Benjie and his grand-dad sat by the pond.
"Look at that big fellow," said Grand-dad. "He's a giant compared to that little guy swimming next to him."
Benjie leaned forward.

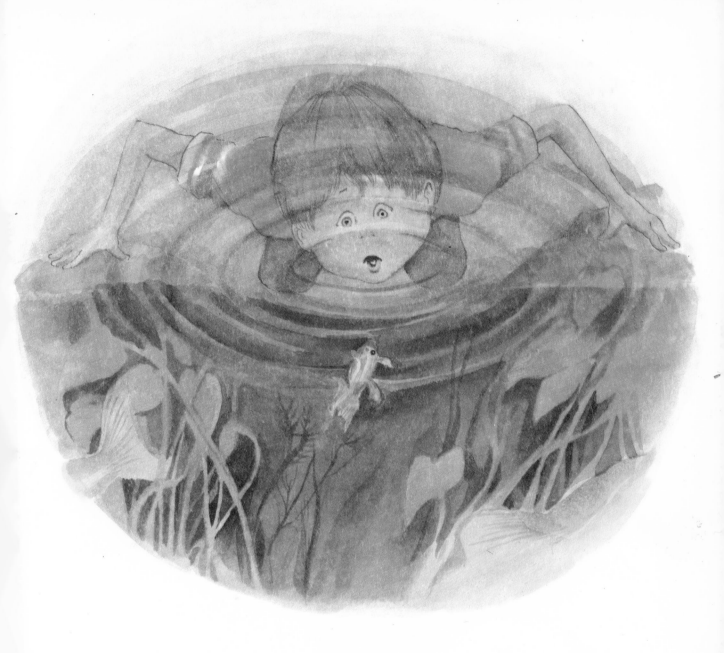

He wasn't looking at the big fish.
He was looking at the little one.
He was looking at the little blue dot
over the little one's right eye.
"That's Goldie!" he hollered.
"I'd know her anywhere."

Grand-dad stared at the little fish. "It's hard to believe," he said. "But I guess it's possible."

Benjie jumped up. "Do you think The Botanical Garden will give her back to me? She *is* mine. Who should I go talk to?"

"Wait a minute," said Grand-dad. "Do you really want to do that? Look at her. She looks so happy here. It's a great place. She's with other fish. There's lots of space here for her to swim in. She can get to grow very big, here."

Benjie watched Goldie swimming this way and that. "You know...I think you're right."

They watched Goldie a while more, then went home. Grand-dad stayed for dinner. They told Benjie's mom about finding Goldie, and about Benjie's decision to let her stay at The Botanical Garden.

"It's all just amazing," said Benjie's mom.

"But great!" said Benjie. "I don't know how she got there. But she did it. Boy, wait till I tell Milton about this!"

That night Benjie fell asleep smiling, thinking about
Goldie. It's true. She did seem pretty happy there.

When he was really all better, which happened very soon, Benjie often went to The Botanical Garden, to see how Goldie was doing, though it was hard to find her sometimes, among all those other goldfish.

MORE ABOUT GOLDFISH

- A goldfish is a type of carp.

- They need shade because they have no eyelids.

- Hundreds of years ago, goldfish were bred in China and Japan from plain-colored carp.

- In the United States, goldfish are raised in goldfish farms.

- A goldfish can live to be 50 years old and get to be one foot long.